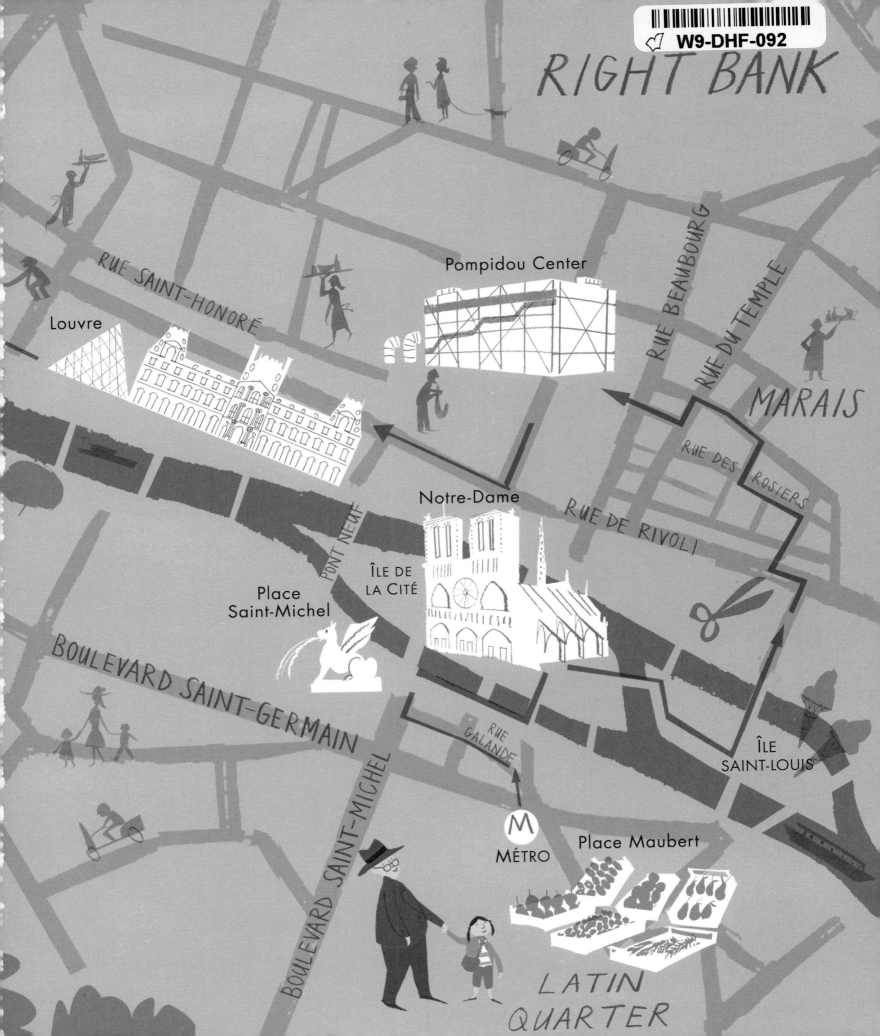

RIGHT BANK

W9-DHF-092

Pompidou Center

Louvre

RUE SAINT-HONORÉ

RUE BEAUBOURG

RUE DU TEMPLE

MARAIS

RUE DES ROSIERS

Notre-Dame

RUE DE RIVOLI

PONT NEUF

ÎLE DE LA CITÉ

Place Saint-Michel

BOULEVARD SAINT-GERMAIN

ÎLE SAINT-LOUIS

RUE GALANDE

BOULEVARD SAINT-MICHEL

M MÉTRO

Place Maubert

LATIN QUARTER

**For Mum and Dad,
Grazia and Vincenzo**

*With special thanks to Billy Rubbino
for the artwork on the last page*

First U.S. edition 2014

Library of Congress Catalog Card Number 2013943083
ISBN 978-0-7636-6984-3

17 18 19 APS 10 9 8 7 6 5 4

Printed in Humen, Dongguan, China

This book was typeset in MKlang Bold and Futura Book.
The illustrations were done in mixed media.

Candlewick Press
99 Dover Street
Somerville, Massachusetts 02144

visit us at www.candlewick.com

CANDLEWICK PRESS

# A WALK IN PARIS

### Salvatore Rubbino

Place Maubert is in the Latin Quarter of Paris, south of the river Seine.

You can buy tickets for the Métro at any station. Some shops and newspaper stands sell them as well.

Another name for Paris is the City of Light.

The Métro is Paris's subway system.

METRO

Maubert Mutualité

LE METRO DE PARIS

**Hello!** This is **me** and that's my grandpa—and we're in *Paris!*

Café METRO

We've just come up from the Métro at **Place Maubert!**

I wonder what all those crates are for. "You'll see," Grandpa promises with a smile.

7

Merci, Monsieur.
Au revoir!

Also a crab,
s'il vous plaît.

Stallholders at a market
know a lot about food
and how to cook it.

Place Maubert is
home to one of Paris's
oldest street markets.

BRASSERIE

PLACE MAUBERT

*Bonjour, Madame!*

*Merci!*

The crates are full of fruit and vegetables!
It's market day in the square.

"Shoppers like to visit their favorite stalls," Grandpa says,
"chatting and asking questions while they choose."

Mmm . . . I get some tasty cheese to try!

Here are some handy
French words and phrases:
*s'il vous plaît* means "please,"
*merci* means "thank you,"
*bonjour* means "hello," and
*au revoir* means "good-bye."

Street markets selling the freshest
ingredients are found all over Paris.
They open on different days, so if
you want to visit one, you need
to check the schedule first!

## We walk down a street where the houses lean together . . .

CREPES

VINS

In medieval times, stone for building was mined from under the city. The mining left behind 180 miles (300 kilometers) of underground tunnels.

In the nineteenth century, the emperor of France asked Baron Georges Haussmann to rebuild Paris. Haussmann designed wide, straight boulevards, where all the roofs and balconies line up. He also improved Paris's water supply and sewage system and created beautiful parks.

fruits de Mer

to one where they stand apart!
"This kind of road is much newer,"
Grandpa tells me. "It's called a boulevard."

It's really wide and busy. We'd better cross
quickly, before the lights change!

Meet you
at Place
Saint-Michel!

GRAND BAR

I see a street cleaner turn a big key.
Now there's water gushing out of the curb!
"Watch your feet, Grandpa!" I say.

"We have these special taps all over Paris,"
the other street cleaner explains. "They give us water
for cleaning, right on the street."

Sculpted fountains called Wallace fountains
are a familiar sight in Paris, positioned on
busy sidewalks and in squares. Throughout
the summer, they provide clean drinking
water to anyone who needs it.

Parisian street cleaners wear green
uniforms and drive green vans.
Even their brooms are green!

Paris has two water systems.
Water for drinking and water for
cleaning run through separate pipes.

The boulevard leads to a square where lots of people are greeting one another. "This is a famous spot," says Grandpa.

The Latin Quarter has been a home to students since the Middle Ages. Paris's university, the old Sorbonne, was founded in this area and dates from the thirteenth century.

Good friends in France might exchange three or four cheek kisses when they meet— or they might shake hands.

Salut!

Bonjour!

Salut!

Bonjour!

Salut!

"People often meet their friends by the fountain at PLACE SAINT-MICHEL."

Place Saint-Michel stands at the heart of the Latin Quarter.

*Salut* is a more casual word for hello.

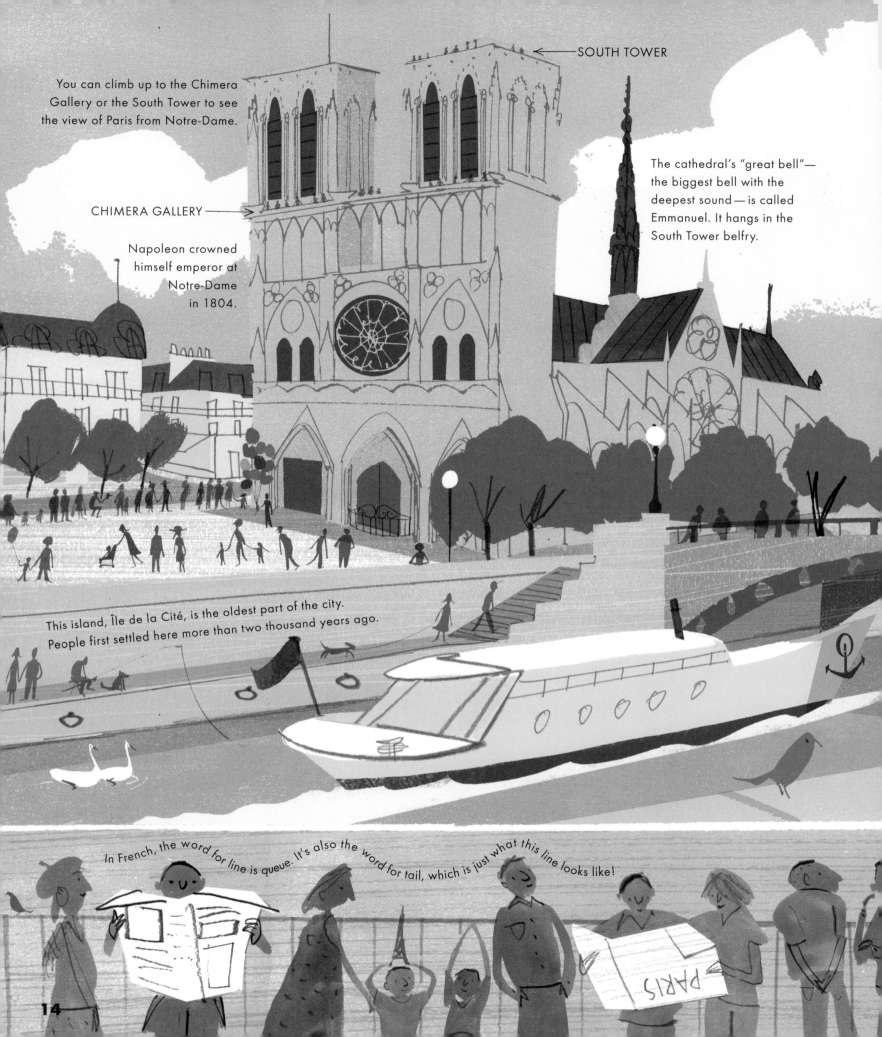

SOUTH TOWER

You can climb up to the Chimera Gallery or the South Tower to see the view of Paris from Notre-Dame.

CHIMERA GALLERY —→

Napoleon crowned himself emperor at Notre-Dame in 1804.

The cathedral's "great bell"— the biggest bell with the deepest sound — is called Emmanuel. It hangs in the South Tower belfry.

This island, Île de la Cité, is the oldest part of the city. People first settled here more than two thousand years ago.

In French, the word for line is queue. It's also the word for tail, which is just what this line looks like!

PARIS

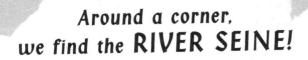

Around a corner,
we find the RIVER SEINE!

"What's that big church on the island?" I ask.

"The Cathedral of Notre-Dame," Grandpa replies. "Would
you like to climb up and see the view?"

I would!

Book stalls have lined
the river since the
mid-sixteenth century.

We have to wait in line for quite a long time. . . .

but it's worth it!
It's lovely and breezy up here.

EIFFEL TOWER

Thirty-seven bridges
cross the river Seine in Paris.
The oldest is Pont Neuf.

LES INVALIDES

ARC DE TRIOMP

RIVER SEINE

These statues of beasts
are called chimeras. They're
made up of body parts from
different creatures!

Notre-Dame's Chimera Gallery is 151 feet (46 meters) above the ground.

Grandpa points out some landmarks. The tallest building we can see is the Eiffel Tower.

SACRÉ-CŒUR

MONTMARTRE

SAINTE-CHAPELLE

SAINT JACQUES TOWER

LOUVRE

It took almost two hundred years to build Notre-Dame.

The part of Paris south of the river is called the Left Bank. The part north of the river is called the Right Bank.

**We make our way back down to the ground**

The bigger island is Île de la Cité.

Visitors tour the river on big boats called *bateaux-mouches*.

The French flag is known as the *Tricolore*, which means "three colors"— blue, white, and red.

BATEAUX-MOUCHES

and over another bridge.

Île Saint-Louis is famous for its ice-cream parlors.

"Paris has two islands," Grandpa explains. "This is the little one, Île Saint-Louis,"

We take a seat close to the water's edge. A boat passes by, so I wave. "Careful!" Grandpa laughs. "Don't fall in!"

Next we cross over to the Right Bank of the river. "Paris has *style*, don't you think?" Grandpa asks as we pass a fancy salon.

I think there are lots of ways to wear your hair!

Chic is another word for stylish.

21 COIFFEUR 21

Paris is a center for fashion.
Haute couture clothes are made to measure
rather than bought in a store.

The poodle is often thought
of as France's national dog.

No wonder I'm hungry. It's one o'clock!
We find a cozy BISTRO for lunch.

Plats du Jour

entrées
Plats
Desserts

A plat du jour is the chef's special dish of the day.

Parisian waiters are highly trained professionals.

Steak-frites, or steak with French fries, is a popular bistro choice.

Most cafés and restaurants in Paris are happy to welcome dogs.

22

A bistro is a small restaurant, often family-run, that serves traditional food.

A brasserie also serves traditional food, but it is usually much bigger than a bistro.

*A little red wine.*

*Merci, Monsieur.*

BOULANGERIE 31

Then we're ready to explore the Marais.

This is a GIANT doorway!

"It has to be wide enough for a horse and carriage," Grandpa explains. "That's how people traveled years ago."

We turn down one street after another

Beigels & Pletzels

The Marais was once a marshland. Now it is a fashiona part of the city, full of shops, cafés, and restaurants.

Chez Marianne

and I think
we might
be lost . . .

← Place des VOSGES

Musée PICASSO

Musée CARNAVALET

Hôtel de SULLY

Centre POMPIDOU →

until Grandpa points to
a strange-looking building.

"Here
we are.
Let's go
around the
front," he says.

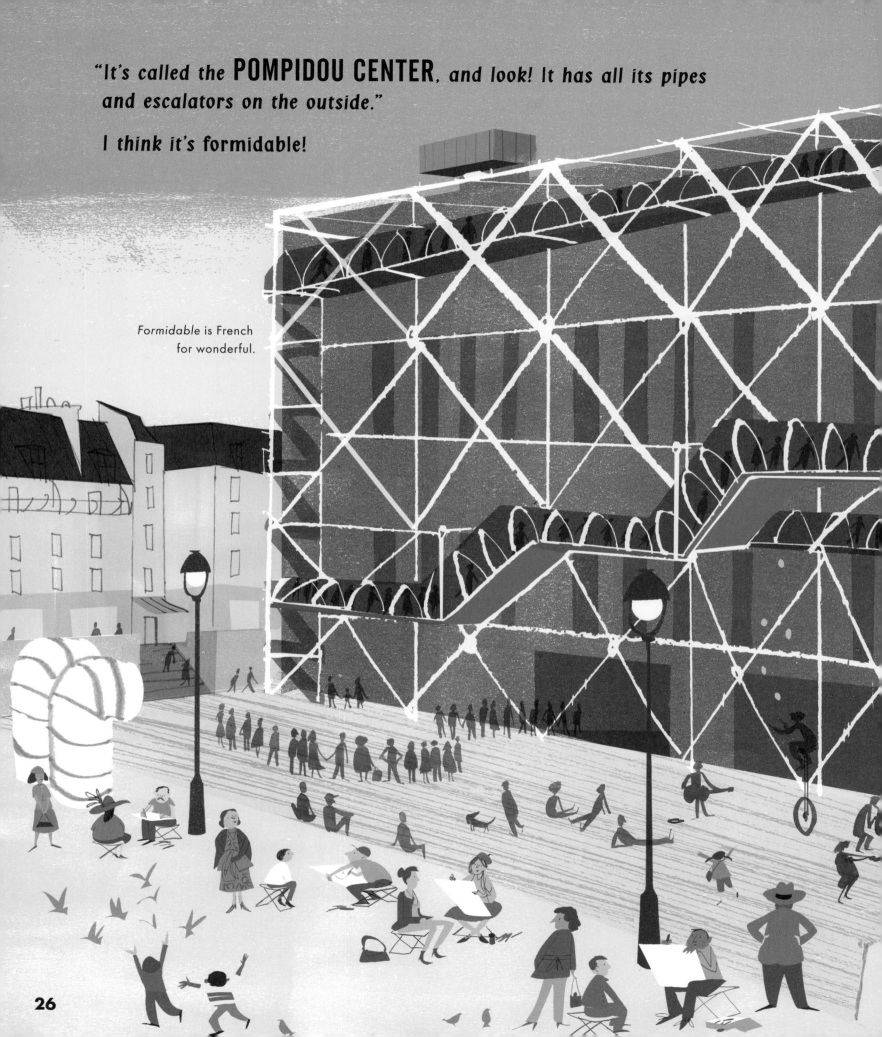

"It's called the **POMPIDOU CENTER**, and look! It has all its pipes
and escalators on the outside."

**I think it's formidable!**

Formidable is French
for wonderful.

The Pompidou Center is a famous gallery for modern art.

Important parts of the building are color-coded. Escalator shafts and elevators are painted red.

The architect's idea was to help people understand how a building works.

Sometimes artists work outside the Pompidou, drawing portraits on the pavement.

27

Cafés are an important part of Paris life.
They often have tables on the sidewalk.

We've walked a long way on a wide, busy road when we come to a window full of cakes!

"Which one would you like?" asks Grandpa.

"Ummm . . . That one, that one, that one . . . and . . .

This kind of shop is a *pâtisserie*, a specialist bakery selling pastries and cakes.

Every tart, profiterole, and éclair is created by a master pastry chef.

28

"THAT one!"
I say.

The Mona Lisa is one of Leonardo da Vinci's best-known paintings. Her eyes are said to follow you around the room.

Napoleon liked the picture so much that he hung it in his bedroom!

**We turn into a courtyard with a pyramid in the middle! There are rows of tall, fancy buildings around the sides.**

The museum is housed in the buildings of an ancient palace.

MONA LISA

The main entrance to the Louvre is through the glass pyramid! Visitors take an elevator or staircase down to a hall, then choose which building to enter from underground.

The pyramid, and the little pyramids next to it, are made of glass and steel. They were built in 1989.

A tour guide is talking to her group. "This is the LOUVRE MUSEUM," she says. "Its treasures include a famous painting called the Mona Lisa."

"I see the Mona Lisa!" I tell Grandpa. "She's on that poster over there!"

# We rest in the Tuileries Gardens.
## Grandpa enjoys his favorite view . . .

The view is of the Triumphal Way, which is 5½ miles (9 kilometers) long and runs in a straight line through Paris.

Two important sites along the route are Place de la Concorde, with its obelisk, and the Arc de Triomphe.

## while I make a friend by the water.

*Boules* is a classic French game. Each player tries to throw his *boule* as close as he can to the little one.

The first manned hydrogen balloon took off from the Tuileries Gardens in 1783. At least half the population of Paris turned out to witness its flight.

Tile-making workshops (*tuileries*) occupied this piece of land until the mid-sixteenth century, when it was turned into a formal garden by Catherine de Médicis.

MÉTRO

**Then Grandpa says we need to find a Métro station.**

You can drag your chair wherever you want in the Tuileries Gardens.

Every spring and fall, the gardens are planted with up to 70,000 plants and bulbs.

The head gardener checks that all the flowering plants are between 27½ inches (70 centimeters) and four feet (1.2 meters) high.

The trees in the Tuileries Gardens are trimmed regularly to keep the view clear.

SORTIE

PLACE DE LA CONCORDE
CÔTÉ JARDIN DES TUILERIES

The first Métro line in Paris
was opened in 1900.

The word *métro* is short
for *métropolitain*.

Some of the
Métro trains have
rubber wheels,
which makes
them feel
bouncy inside.

Paris has the
second busiest
subway system
in Europe, after
Moscow.

016

101

We listen to a cheerful tune while we wait for our train.

"Where are we going?" I ask, but he won't tell me! "It's a surprise," he says.

The sky's getting dark when
we come up from the Métro.
Grandpa buys me a souvenir
from a kiosk by the station.

The word *souvenir*
also means a memory
in French.

"Do you remember the Eiffel Tower?" he asks me.
"We saw it from Notre-Dame."

I look up . . .

Double-decker elevators carry visitors to the top.

At 1,063 feet (324 meters) including the spire, the Eiffel Tower is the tallest building in Paris.

The Eiffel Tower was built by Gustave Eiffel and completed in 1889. The construction was a feat of engineering, taking only two years, two months, and five days.

The Eiffel Tower sways a little in strong winds. It can also grow taller or shorter by up to 6 inches (15 centimeters) depending on the temperature.

A beacon of light sweeps across Paris from the top of the tower.

The Eiffel Tower is bathed in golden light from dusk onward. Then, for five minutes at the start of every hour, 20,000 extra lightbulbs sparkle on and off!

**...and find myself face to face with the real Eiffel Tower! It's enormous and fizzing with lights!**

Since the 1960s, the tower has been painted light brown to match its surroundings. Its earlier colors have included deep red and canary yellow.

The tower weighs 10,100 tons.

Many of Paris's monuments, churches, statues, fountains, and bridges are lit up at night.

We stay till the end of the show.

"Can we come back one day?" I ask Grandpa as we leave.

"I'd like that," he says.

"When I get home," I tell him, "I'll make a souvenir for you. Then you'll always remember our walk in Paris."

Merci
and au revoir!

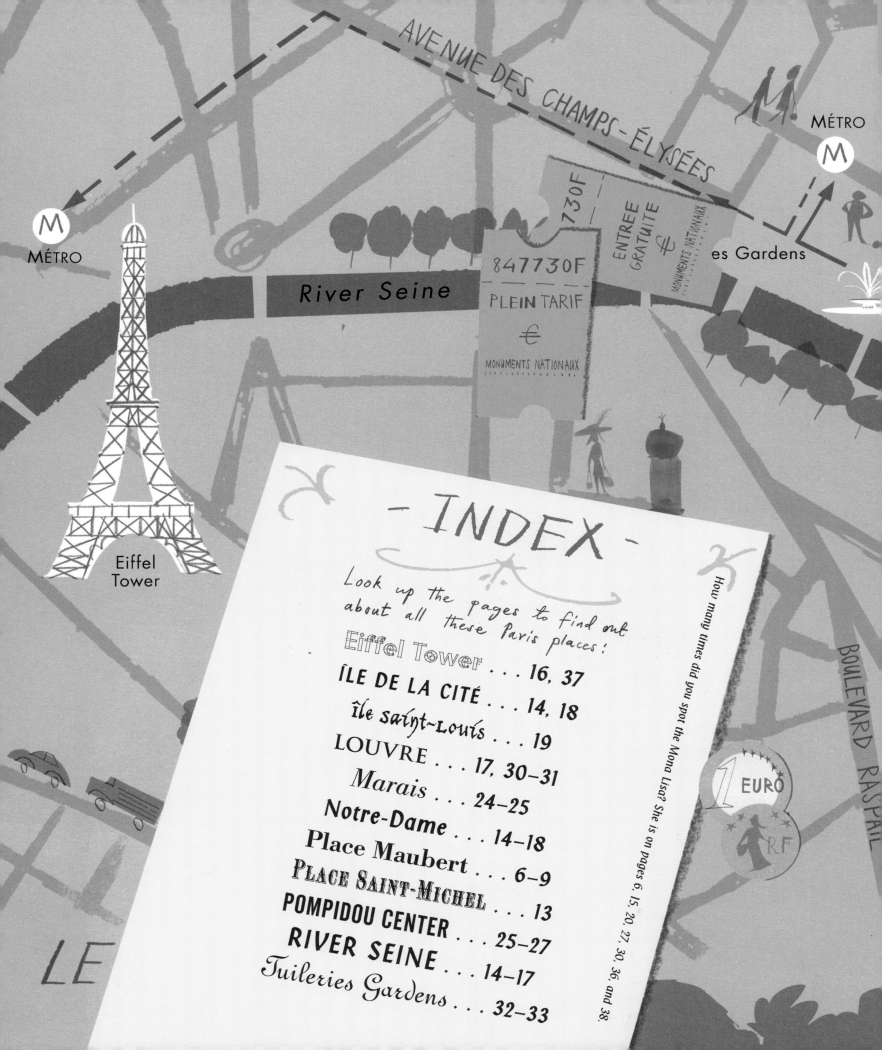

AVENUE DES CHAMPS-ÉLYSÉES

MÉTRO M

MÉTRO M

MÉTRO

Eiffel Tower

River Seine

es Gardens

730F

847730F

PLEIN TARIF

€

MONUMENTS NATIONAUX

ENTRÉE GRATUITE €

MONUMENTS NATIONAUX

BOULEVARD RASPAIL

LE

1 EURO

RF

How many times did you spot the Mona Lisa? She is on pages 6, 15, 20, 27, 30, 36, and 38.

# - INDEX -

Look up the pages to find out about all these Paris places!